Farm Fun

Farm Jobs

by Tessa Kenan

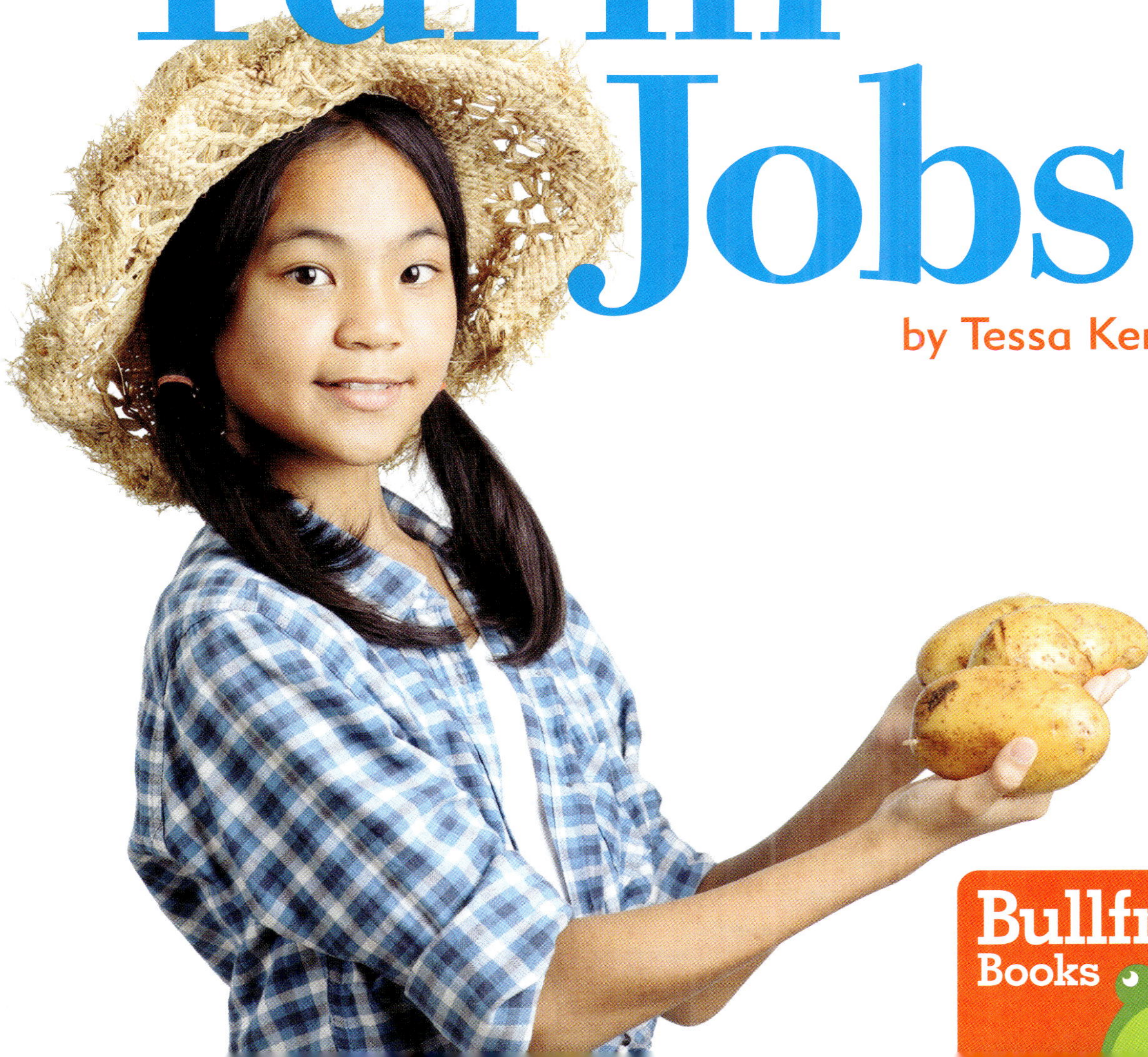

Bullfrog Books

Ideas for Parents and Teachers

Bullfrog Books let children practice reading informational text at the earliest reading levels. Repetition, familiar words, and photo labels support early readers.

Before Reading

- Discuss the cover photo. What does it tell them?
- Look at the picture glossary together. Read and discuss the words.

Read the Book

- "Walk" through the book and look at the pictures. Let the child ask questions. Point out the photo labels.
- Read the book to the child, or have him or her read independently.

After Reading

- Prompt the child to think more. Ask: Farmers have a lot of important jobs. Do you want to work on a farm?

Bullfrog Books are published by Jump!
5357 Penn Avenue South
Minneapolis, MN 55419
www.jumplibrary.com

Library of Congress Cataloging-in-Publication Data

Names: Kenan, Tessa, author.
Title: Farm jobs / Tessa Kenan.
Description: Minneapolis, MN: Jump!, Inc., [2021]
Series: Farm fun | Includes index.
Audience: Ages 5–8 | Audience: Grades K–1
Identifiers: LCCN 2019053337 (print)
LCCN 2019053338 (ebook)
ISBN 9781645275237 (hardcover)
ISBN 9781645275244 (ebook)
Subjects: LCSH: Farm life—Juvenile literature.
Farmers—Juvenile literature.
Classification: LCC S521 .K44 2021 (print)
LCC S521 (ebook) | DDC 630—dc23
LC record available at https://lccn.loc.gov/2019053337
LC ebook record available at https://lccn.loc.gov/2019053338

Editor: Jenna Gleisner
Designer: David Stavitzski

Photo Credits: Iryna_Shmihel/Shutterstock, cover; OHishiapply/Shutterstock, 1; Anatta_Tan/Shutterstock, 3; SimplyDay/Shutterstock, 4 (background); Ariel Skelley/Getty, 4 (foreground), 5, 22tl; Jürgen Fälchle/Alamy, 6–7 (background), 23tl; PattyPhoto/Shutterstock, 6–7 (foreground); Sumetee Theesungnern/EyeEm/Getty, 8–9, 22bl, 23br; Marc Venema/Shutterstock, 9; Countrypixel/Adobe Stock, 10; Heide Benser/Getty, 11; oticki/Shutterstock, 12–13, 16, 22tr, 23bl, 22br; Sergei Butorin/Shutterstock, 14–15; Bryan Eastham/Shutterstock, 17; Rido/Shutterstock, 18–19; Lightfield Studios/Adobe Stock, 20–21; robert cicchetti/Shutterstock, 23tr; Vishnevskiy Vasily/Shutterstock, 24.

Printed in the United States of America at Corporate Graphics in North Mankato, Minnesota.

Table of Contents

Hard Workers 4
Many Jobs 22
Picture Glossary 23
Index 24
To Learn More 24

Hard Workers

This farmer is up early. Why?

The animals are hungry!
She feeds them.

The chickens are up, too!

The farmer lets them out of their coop.

The coop keeps them safe at night.

coop

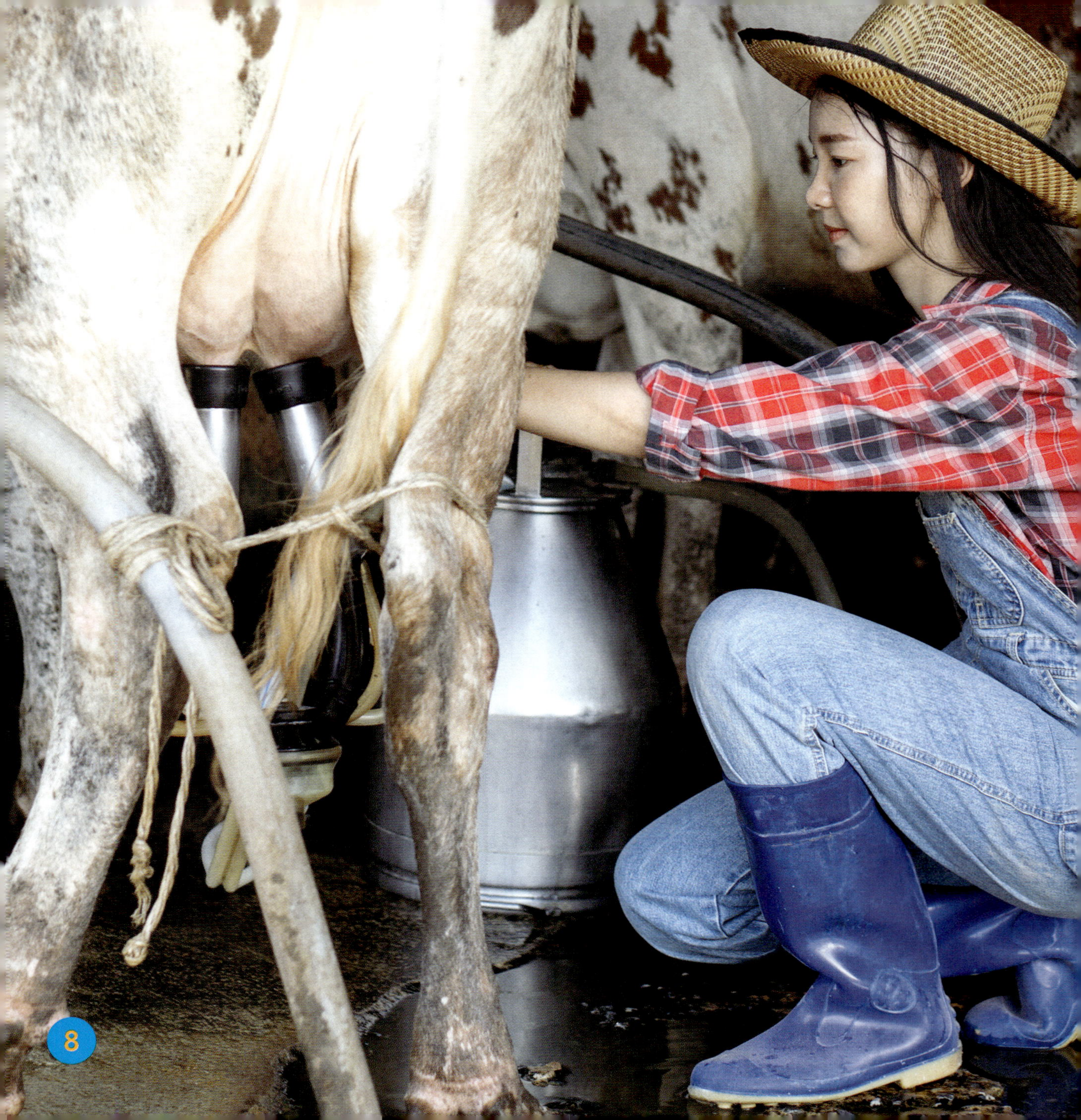

This farmer milks cows.

Cool!

This sow has piglets.

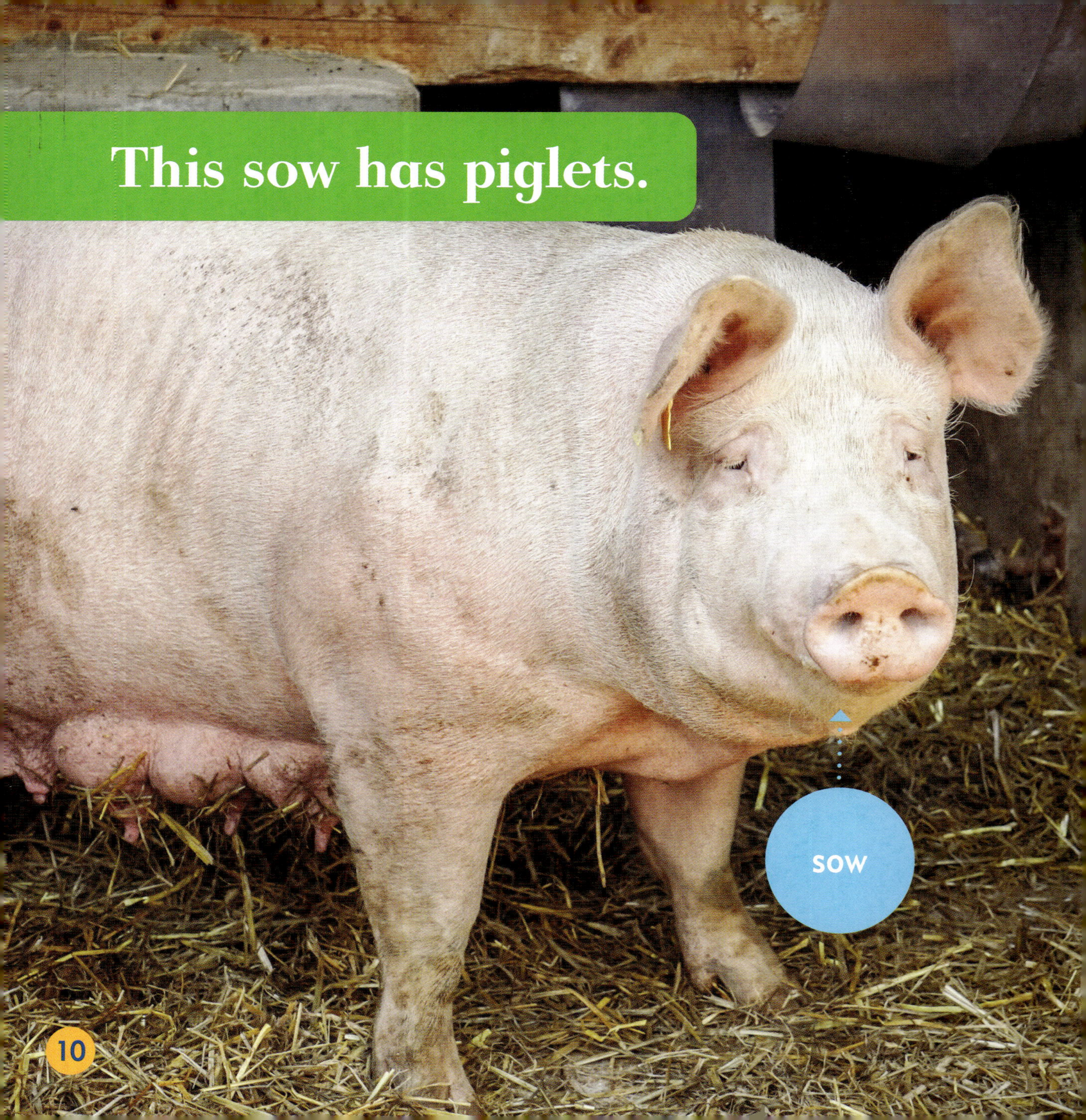

The farmer helps.

Cute!

Time to get in the tractor!

There are crops to plant.

The farmer spends
his days in the field.

tractor

Oh, no!

The tractor broke down.

That is OK.

The farmer can fix it!

In fall, he harvests the crops.

He works late!

Farmers have a lot of jobs.
They are all important!

Do you want to do farm jobs?

Many Jobs

Farmers have many jobs! These are just some. Can you think of others?

feeding
Farmers feed farm animals in the morning and at night.

harvesting
Farmers with crops harvest them in fall after they have grown all summer.

milking
Farmers with dairy cows milk them in the morning and at night.

planting
Farmers with crops plant seeds in the spring.

Picture Glossary

coop
A small building or pen that houses chickens or other small animals.

crops
Plants grown for food.

harvests
Gathers crops from a field.

milks
Takes milk from a cow or other animal.

Index

chickens 6
coop 6
cows 9
crops 12, 16
feeds 5
fix 15
harvests 16
milks 9
piglets 10
plant 12
tractor 12, 15
works 17

To Learn More

Finding more information is as easy as 1, 2, 3.

1. Go to www.factsurfer.com
2. Enter "farmjobs" into the search box.
3. Click the "Surf" button to see a list of websites.